Halloween, Fireside
or Just Plain
Weird

Poems

E S Cuny

Kallisto Gaia Press Inc.
801 E. 51st. Street
Suite 365-246
Austin TX 78723
Phone (254) 654-7205
www.Kallistogaiapress.org

Cover photo: E.S. Cuny
Abandoned Manyunk Property, Phila. PA

ISBN: 978-1-952224-15-7

Thank you Sallie,
and the others.

Table of Contents

Some Lite Ones

The Old Man Who Snored Too Loud

(Children's Verse Dept.)

Dust stirred in the attic
of the Old Man's house.
Then panes rattled in windows,
and cups clattered in cupboards.
The dog covered his ears with his paws
and started a low howl. The cat left.
The crickets outside got quiet.
Neighborhood dogs joined in the howling.
Then the neighbors themselves got up
because the noise was so great
they thought it was an earthquake!
They gathered outside then went up to the house.
Worried about the Old Man they knocked
and knocked and knocked and rang the bell,
and began shouting for the Old Man Grandpa
to see if he was all right. But they banged
on the door so hard it opened up
and finally they just went in and –
Boy! Were they surprised! Because you know
that Grandpa who snored too loud?
It wasn't him! It was his own
Grand-kid –
　　　(Who looks a lot like you!)

THERE'S A FOX IN THE HOUSE

In downy ruffs diaper fluffs
hens remove to upper lower shelves are
tiers cleared
squawking squealing
claws scritching feet sliding
feathers a flutter clothes
unfurled hurled
wings beating arms whirling leading
as soft steps sneaking little paws picking
nose around without a sound thru what in pantry's found
tiny sharp teeth suddenly strike dexterous fingers
a flash of fright flick flashlight
leaving behind trailing a line
splotches of blood, broken bones, of mechanical parts, cookie crumbs,
straw scattered paper shredded
from nests upset baskets turned over
litter left all over the floor ...

as Chaos replaces order.

Look out! A certain Mr. Fox is in the house!

THE FAIRY HOUSE UNSEEN

While riding on the bus down Duval Street
I glanced at a house from my window seat,
a house that seemed 'bout a half block over,
a building I'd never noticed before.

It stood away from the others about two stories tall,
canting off of plumb, with a balcony over all.
A most curious house, as if from a mythical tale:
sharply pitched roof, dormers, and a gingerbread rail.
All seen in a moment way too brief,
then the sight cut off as we lurched down the street.

Though I've looked from that route many times since,
and on foot poked behind every garden and fence,
that house that I saw – I saw it, I swear! –
it's gone, gone ... it's just not there.
No two storied house, nor apartment or garage;
just a mind playing shadows, or a Fairy's mirage?

PALACE SHADES PARK

While walking up to get my car in the parking garage,
where the old Armadillo Headquarters had stood
– a demolished Rock 'n Roll Palace that I wish redone
if only there was someway, somehow, that maybe it could.

A VW van coughed as it passed me by
on its way up looking for a place to park.
Tinny doors slammed and hand in hand
a couple walked down from out of the dark.

He had a pony tail and goatee, and wore
sandals and jeans and a tie-dyed shirt;
she had boots and bracelets, a cowboy hat
and a tied-dyed top with a beaded skirt.

They crossed over in front of me
as I followed the ramp up and around.
They continued chatting eagerly,
passing me by on their way down.

While he was busy with some explanation
she laughed and tossed her long blonde hair.
I looked back in a sudden inclination
just as she cast at me a quizzical stare.

I got in my car, paid at the exit bar, then curious,
drove around searching for them all over everywhere.
I was at first surprised until I realized, they were gone
– figments that had vanished into the thin air.

Ode to Cernan
(And the Others)

He was the twelfth and last man to walk off the moon,
and in one giant step for a man, too soon
he sighed as his left foot lifted from its dusty perch,
swung in an arc, and landed back on Earth.
Mission Apollo was over far and away before its time,
one fleeting step back, for all mankind.

The Man in the Moon watched warily, and unseen by them,
duffled his dreams, slid up the steps and slipped inside the LEM.
He left behind the Rabbit because he wanted to find out,
how real gravity felt, and what that blue was all about.
He wanted to breathe in air under skies he'd barely seen,
and understand the intricacies of the color green.

But now at night, deep in slumber, do their spirits each hover
        over,
searching for the moon in the man, on the face of the other?

Long Black Shadow

There is a long black shadow thrown deep in outer space,
it happens when the Earth and Moon converge in their solar trace.
Though each one throws a cone of dark, alone they're easily diffused;
but when a lunar eclipse crowns, a darker shaft will merge from two.

That's a hint that our planet has a moon – if seen from far away.
Is this the only sign of possible life, in which we have no say?
For a moon gives the probability there's a spot where things can grow,
and counter mad old entropy, safe in a spiral arm hidden and remote.

It took billions of years to get us here placed in this special setting,
where intelligence could arise and thrive a-midst a living heaven.
So what madness is this to let things run amiss, while knowledge we
forswear
– we may not be able to live in peace but we can't survive without
clean air.

We're turning the oceans into deserts, squandering what gifts
were given,
are we sending a warning to the Heavens, not to ever try this again?
By giving up the substance of consciousness to ignorance and greed,
bleached bones on a barren shore will be our only destiny.

Unless, of course, we decide to fulfill the promise and care,
that life of Gaia will continue on, and not become a sterile affair.
Can a regeneration reach across nations to share the task of healing?
It's the only way that in time we may claim our right to celestial being.

Will that beam then carry our story of grace through the Universe,
proclaiming we found our way, to let life flourish here on Earth;
or will the message that's delivered be but the death-knell of our fate?
For that is our long black shadow that we cast deep into outer space.

Some Not So Lite

Flcik'ring Shadows

I. Incursion

And I have sensed death approaching, coming up the stairs
seeking out my presence, watched him enter into my room,
swirling in on darkness, inquiring of my health, wondering
if the time was right, twirling out his cloak of doom.
I tried to get up to greet him but the room began to spin,
sweat was pouring from my brow, my heart began to pound.
In fevered anxiety I said, "How dare you, I need a little more."
With fearful haughtiness I sent him away, though I wasn't sound.
I was relieved but spent, and astounded at his seeming arrogance;
Yet in reflection, I think it was more a gracious act of benevolence.

II. Aftermath

Yet it's not like he's left me alone. He just waits, patiently.
I glimpse him in shadow plays that take away my complacency:
when something moves in the peripheral that's not really there;
when a figure forms from little more than mere motes floating in air,
figures that flicker just long enough to draw my attention,
but fade into nothingness when brought into my vision.
Then shadows tumble in the halls at night, where no footsteps fall,
or branches scratch at the window pane, when there is no wind at all;
they seem to be fingers beckoning to where, with a sketchy bow,
he's inviting, by asking the eternal question: Are you ready now?

How a Ghost Sees Things

I blend in and then out among the fog and mists
everything, it seems is so damned vaporous,
which makes my existence a constant horror
when I can't even see myself in a mirror.

It's awfully hard to grasp things, not just objects
but even the simplest of ideas and concepts
such as, Where am I?, or, What is that?, yet nothing is clear.
The questions drift off unanswered, and I'm still here.

As for sustenance I'm actually OK, you see
the vapors from empty bottles belong to me.
The same is true of the sizzles from a grill
or the aromas wafting from a baker's window sill.

The Hell of it is I still reach out to grab and snatch
only to hit a mental wall with a soul shaking *smack!*
And I have to face up, over and over, yet again
I'm not here at all, and fade back, away, just a whim.

I can't stand the sun, though I don't know why.
Can't stand any water, makes me want to cry.
Can't stand the night, though I can finally be seen
sometimes, in the misty vapors of your dreams.

Don't know why I try putting this into those wisps,
they won't hold what I write, and you can't read it.

At the Mermaid Bar and Grill

She met me at her table.
Neon red and blue pulsating outside
She was spinning a shell,

A pendant dangling luxuriously
Held within a breastly gasp: Nothing is true.
She met me at the table.

Though being and description
Are but a net of words, she played life the way
She was spinning her shell.

Precarious the tongue that does not behold
The windy waves of meaning, such as,
She met me at her table.

But atop the winding staircase
Blue and green shadows led beyond red curtains where
She was spinning her shell.

Consider not the coral brainy,
Nor the Mother of Pearl there inlaid.
Merely: She met me at the table;
Where she was spinning her shell.

The Dolce Vita Arbiters

Some think it was just
a bistro,
the old Dolce Vita,
but in fact it was where
the arbiters of values,
in this world, met.

(They were)
young women who sat
at tables,
who set the lines
amid the talk of girls.

That is, as long as they
didn't know it.
(But)
once realized,
they aged out,
and that power forfeit.

Not unlike
the Dolce Vita itself.

So We Set Out

So the three of us set out on a Sunday morning
looking for breakfast but found ourselves roaming
on what had become our customary trek,
but I now with a bandaged neck –
where the razor'd missed but bit too deep;
she with makeup heavy on cheeks
a little smeared and hastily applied,
and sunglasses covering puffy eyes;
and he in long sleeves, cuffs buttoned tight
covering his wrists which he kept out of sight,
unanalogous in this morning's unholy sweltering.

So we set out though my throat was festering,
and her stomach still wobbly from all the pills,
and he'd given up on all his "catechism's shills,"
as he called it, but none of us really gave a shit,
we just sleepwalked in steps by force of habit.

So once again we set out for a Sunday breakfast
or just a place – any place – that would have us.
Each of us had risen only to find
no one had come to replace us in kind.
No one had even tried give us a warning:
that we'd wake madder'n Jesus on Monday morning.

So we set out, for a place that doesn't exist,
a place – any place – serving a breakfast
in this God-forsaken blast furnace forming ...
on this, the Sunday of Sundays' mornings.

WHEN IT'S GETTIN' HOT IN TEXAS

Well, when it's getting' hot in Texas
and climbs past 90 degrees
you can bet your boots spring has sprung
and there won't be another freeze.

Now your own body's temperature
is around ninety-eight-point-six,
and as a thermometer rises up
your sweat begins to fizz.

And a funny thing happens when that heat
goes up and past your own –
your body well melt, your hands will float
and you'll think your mind has flown.

And as that outside temp keeps climbing
and goes past a'hunert and eight,
a funny thing happens in that heat –
your soul can evaporate.

It's a phenomenon not unknown to man
so be careful of triple digits,
if you don't hang on to your shadow's grip
you're in danger of losing it.

Now some say the same thing happens
when you're hiking out on treks,
or if you've been running a marathon mile
and you're deep into your klicks.

The difference with the heat is,
sometimes you don't even know
until the chills come over you –
that's when Death will swoop in low.

You desperately need to find a way
to cool your body down,
for if there is no water or shade
you might end up underground.

And sometimes there's just nothing,
no, nothing close at hand.
You can fall on your knees, beg the Lord please,
but you're headed for the promised land.

Yet there's a way to keep your soul intact –
just stop your forlorn quest,
and laugh at this cosmic joke called life
'cause laughter, my friend, is the cooling-est.

Snick! Snick!

I often took my dog in the truck when going to the shop.
She'd jump out of the back of the bed before we'd even stop,
because an Oriental restaurant had opened right next door
and their dumpster had many strange odors she loved to explore.

There was a bus-boy there who cagily enticed her as a friend,
with little treats while chatting her up in his native North Korean.
His job was mainly to take out the trash and sharpen all their knives
  – Snick! Snick! – went the blades as he honed them up-and-down
                                                          their sides.

He'd sit out there in the back among razor-edges on concrete steps
– Snick! Snick! – went the steel as he puffed along on his cigarettes.
He might give a whistle, or hum to himself or even sing a little riff,
so she would come over and nudge up close, for a snuffle and a sniff.

But seeing me come around looking for her, he'd stare away
                                              beyond our roofs;
dreaming of home and his mother's own, Dwag-Pawl Soup?
                                              – Snick! Snick!

The End

Eugene writes this for you from Austin TX, and hopes you have enjoyed a sense of unworldliness, a touch of the macabre, or at least some bit of humor, light or dark, found inside. Comments always appreciated at: ifandorx9@gmail.com.

Thank you – E.C.